THE BROKEN HEART

Lilia Isar
The Broken Heart

All rights reserved
Copyright © 2024 by Lilia Isar

No part of this publication may be reproduced, distributed, or transmitted in any form or by any means, including photocopying, recording, or other electronic or mechanical methods, without the prior written permission of the publisher, except in the case of brief quotations embodied in critical reviews and certain other noncommercial uses permitted by copyright law.

—

Published by - Spines
ISBN: 979-8-89569-053-6

THE BROKEN HEART

Lilia Isar

Contents

About the Author

I was born in the Soviet Union and at the age of 15 immigrated with the youth movement "Naale 16" to Israel. I came without knowing a family, money, or knowledge of Hebrew and the only possessions I had were a small suitcase, the spirit of Zionism, and a strong connection to this land. I studied in "Nir HaEmek" boarding school, graduated from Tel Aviv University, the faculty of human science, and have a teacher's license from the Lewinsky college of education. I work as an English teacher, give lectures and share my story to inspire and give hope to others. In recent years, after experiencing a strong mental crisis myself, I felt the urge to share my personal experiences since my very childhood in communism and till my immigration and life in Israel; when the war broke, I decided to dedicate this book to the soldiers of Israel. The book is based on my personal fascinating biography and all the characters are based on real people, some of whom I didn't meet in person, including my great grandfathers and the victims of the war "The Iron Swords". I also intertwined moving Kabbalistic and spiritual messages, including the sources, personal interpretations, and experiences. The book is pierced with the Jewish and Zionist spirit and all the characters have one thing in common-the broken heart, which is deeply inspired by the Rabbi and kabbalist Menachem Mendel of Kotz's quote: "

There is nothing so whole as the broken heart", because only the broken, a sensitive and defenseless heart can include all hearts in the world and become whole again.

Only the broken heart can really feel compassion and sympathy, thus opening itself to others and absorbing all hearts in the world.

We Have One Heart!

Introduction

There is a legend that tells us that thousands of years ago we lived like "one man in one heart", but as the pride began to rise, humankind became more and more arrogant and people began to argue one with another; that's how the hatred appeared. As a result, one heart broke into many different pieces that spread around the world; since then we have walked lonely and incomplete, hoping to find the missing pieces some day.

PART ONE

THE BROKEN HEART

THE BROKEN HEART

PART I

The plane took off and Clara realized there was no way back, she had a one-way ticket only. She left behind her past, her family, her friends and didn't know if she would ever see them again. She didn't know anything about the place where she was going but truly believed that there, behind the horizon, a beautiful new life, was waiting just for her. She was traveling to the land promised to her grandfathers, to the land of Israel, meaning in

Hebrew straight to God. She honestly believed that she was traveling to Him and that was enough for her.

As her feet touched the ground, the fear of the unknown, the uncanny, began to disappear. She found courage in her heart and the more courageous she became, the more one universal truth opened to her eyes. That was the beginning of the long journey home.

The train station was full of exotic colors: people wearing black and white clothes that didn't fit the season, women were hurrying to enter baby carriage into the wagon; there was also a group of young people that caught her special attention. This group were soldiers, wearing Israeli uniforms and holding guns, including women. "What a beautiful picture!", thought Clara to herself.

Clara felt warmth and humidity, coming from the trains of the flaming hot Israeli summer. She wanted to buy a drink and as an answer to her thoughts, saw a fridge with ice cream. She took out her purse and pointed to pistachio ice cream, gave money, and returned happily to the same bench, where she left her suitcase.

"So that's the taste of home and this is the promised land where her soul was longing to return for so long", thought Clara to herself. That was not a dream any longer.

Her love affair with this country started long before she knew about its existence. She grew up in a dictatorship that concealed everything, including her real identity and roots; Israel looked just like a tiny dot on the map. But now, when she could see it for real, she realized it had always existed in her heart, a point in her heart, connecting her to the source of everything, the source of creation itself.

Israel was in her blood, her heart and soul, the collective memory of her ancestors that got somehow lost in the desert on their way home. She crossed the continent without money, language, and family just to get here. But God spoke to her in a language that she could understand, she truly believed in omens and signs that the creator delivered to her through the people she met in her life.

She was deeply inside her thoughts when the train arrived. She took out her purse when suddenly realized that she spent all her money on the ice and forgot the change.God is in details: in the green dress she wore on the same day, in the pink lilies that caught her attention and in the crowd of soldiers she saw on the platform; and without any hesitation approached one of them asking him to lend her money. When their eyes met, both realized that it was meant to be.

"How did you recognize me?", asked Clara years later.

"You wore a green dress and high heels, just as it was determined above", answered Michael, the soldier she met at the train station.

Since then, they haven't separated or just for a while.

PART II

Clara didn't choose to be an educator, the profession chose her; looking back she thought it was the mission that unconsciously led her to this country. She felt like she was holding the keys of all hearts and she just had to find the right one to open the child's heart.

She truly believed that this way she was gathering the tiny pieces of the huge heart that was once broken in Babylon. Destiny was sometimes harsh on her but she chose to transform hatred and anger into love and light.

The school's principal met Clara at the station. "Yehezkel, the manager", he introduced himself and added, "You must be very courageous, if you came to teach in a boarding school, without knowing Hebrew and teaching experience in Israel; it's a totally different world from the one you knew".

"Cowardice is one of the biggest vices, if not the biggest", quoted Clara, the masterpiece of Russian author "Master and Margarita" who suffered a lot during his lifetime and whose only wish was to finish his novel before he died. He also wrote about Jerusalem, the spiritual heart on Earth, never visiting the eternal city by himself.

They were traveling through the fields, and the wind was blowing into her face, spreading her hair; but unlike in the past, it felt different. She felt the touch of magic in this land-the sun shined very brightly and the sky was pure and even the air was interwoven with the light of creation. Just like a mother loves unconditionally her child, Clara fell in love with the land of Israel; with all its imperfections, it was perfect for her.

The school building's architecture didn't impress her and the people didn't greet her. But all that didn't matter: *she came home*. She was determined to stay here and nothing could bother her to change her mind.

The Israelis didn't treat her friendly at the beginning, which surprised her. She expected that they would show sympathy and compassion because they shared the same tragic history and the same blood. But Clara knew it was because people were always afraid of the new and different. It was always easier to judge the other than to look deeply into one's soul and to accept. However, she deeply believed that they would see her inner beauty with time and would become part of her heart.

Her students didn't immediately fall in love with her either; they made fun of her accent and sometimes she even felt discriminated against, which was more painful than antisemitism.

"Go back home, this is not Russia ", they used to tell her, which was harsh and cruel. She couldn't get where this hatred came from but wouldn't give it much space in her life.

And one day, the students began to adore Clara, looking for her company outside the classes. They were inspired by her, her love was contagious. She reaped the fruits that she sowed, becoming the center of their Universe.

There also existed a special bondage between her and the student called Miya, whose mother died of cancer a few years ago. Miya's father couldn't absorb the loss or mourn with a little girl in his hands and Miya, who was an artist, found herself in a boarding school. Clara believed that Miya should develop her artistic skills and that one day she might become a famous painter.

Clara also believed that people don't just pass away into nowhere, they disappear from this world to exist in the other. She used to tell Miya that one day her mom would find a way to connect her heart.

"You'll see that one day she'll send you a sign and you will see her in the flowers that will flourish in the early spring, in the sound of the sea foam, or the child laughing with you. I don't know how that will happen and that's the beauty of the uncertainty and trust, but you'll see it happening. I promise".

Days passed after days, stretching into months and soon the year would be over since Clara came to Israel, learned Hebrew, and taught the kids. One day she got an unexpected call, she almost forgot him when she heard Michael's voice.

"Where have you been? I was waiting for so long, losing hope to see you again", Clara was sobbing when she heard him.

"I was constantly looking for you and this time I won't let you go", answered the soldier.

They met in the evening of the same day and had never separated since then. He loved her like nobody did before and she answered him back. Sometimes love comes silently out of nowhere, probably from the same parts that were lost when our hearts broke.

PART III

For most people the sense of vision is taken for granted but it wasn't so for Clara. From the very childhood she had to fight for the right to see the world in all its magnificent shapes and colors. And when such an important sense as vision is impaired, you develop other senses like hearing, smell or touch. But most of all you develop the sense of 'feeling' and the deepest empathy. "There are things worse than physical blindness, the spiritual darkness", she always told to herself.

This year Clara started to lose her vision rapidly. She knew that blindness was just a matter of time–at least, that's what the doctors told her when she began to lose her sight from a young age, probably as a result of an explosion on the atomic station and radiation spreading all over the place. The doctors tried to adjust the proper treatment, but it proved impossible to stop the disease.

Clara had begun to prepare herself for the worst, learning different strategies to stay independent; most of all she feared becoming a burden on someone. She honestly told Michael and he said that it changed nothing, he loved her and will love her forever.

Anyway, he asked her permission to try and find a doctor who might help restore her vision. And he did: the doctor named Ben Haim, returned Clara's life full of joy and happiness. The operation lasted many hours, and ten people that Clara didn't know about were praying for her simultaneously.

Their sincere prayer from the bottom of their broken hearts was so strong that the universe could hear it. This way kindness and generosity Clara was spreading all around her life, found its way back to her. Truly, God shows himself in mysterious ways, she began to see!

"Look how green is the grass and how blue is the sky!" she would shout enthusiastically during the first days of her newly gained life, and only those who hadn't seen the light of the day like her since a young age could understand the feeling, sparkling in her deep green eyes.

Soon Clara and Michael got married. They organized a humble and beautiful marriage in the sunset on the beach. The scarlet sun almost sunk into the royally blue sea, the birds were dancing in a triangle and nature itself blessed their union. The seagull flew in the blue sky and Miya, the student, pointed, shouting happily.

"My mom, she sent me a sign! This is a seagull named Johanat Leviston, who always existed in our hearts. My mom told me that I would see it in the moments of happiness. Now I know for sure she can hear and see me, actually, she never left and was always here", Maya pointed at her heart and added, "It is only with the heart that one can see rightly; what is essential is invisible to the eye", quoted Maya *The Little Prince*.

Clara and Michael lived happily ever after. They had two wonderful daughters and later grandchildren. Clara fulfilled her deepest dream-to light the torch on Israeli Independence Day, the country she loved more than anything else. They shared so much in common. Both Clara and her country survived against all the odds, managed to overcome all challenges and suffering, and blossomed again and again. Just like the birds of Phoenix, they both managed to come back to life and be reborn from the ashes.

When it was time to say goodbye, Michael was holding his loved one, kissing her face and caressing her curls that caught his attention years ago at the train station. "Please don't cry, I couldn't have asked for a better life and I'm leaving whole and happy after I gathered so many hearts. We'll meet again in the next life, I'll give you a sign and you will recognize me again beyond millions of other eyes just like before".

And she disappeared like an angel in eternity and when people came to separate from Clara, they felt like "one man in one heart". She managed to unite them and that was worth her life. All of a sudden, in the middle of a sunny day, it started to rain, leaving a gorgeous rainbow in the sky and only Michael knew that it was her materialization. She came to tell him that she loves him that they will meet soon again and that it will be like that forever because love never disappears, and life is stronger than death.

Love is Forever

CHAPTER 2

WHERE IS MESSIAH?

Sarah was a 91-year-old resident in the retirement home for elderly people in the north of Haifa. She was one of the first pioneers who came illegally to Palestine during the British mandate. She was a Holocaust survivor who miraculously managed to escape the Nazis regime, leaving behind her family in the extermination camps.

She came at the time when the British were drowning the

boats with desperately exhausted people—people who survived the Holocaust were destined to death again. The entire world was against their existence, nobody wanted to accept the Jews.

Luckily, Sarah survived. When she landed on the promised land, she got an orange in one hand, so that she might drink and a shovel in the other, so that she could dig the sand and start building the country. They looked like the living skeletons, starved almost to death, but driven by the spirit of Zionism and determined to build the country of their own.

They were driven by a desperate idea to build the Jewish state and nobody would ever again pull them out of their beds, taking their basic belongings, denying their human rights. They will not be "lamb to the slaughter" again. No country came to protect or defend the Jews openly during WWII and they had no one to rely on but themselves.

The Jews fought for their lives and knew there was no way back. Here, on the land of Israel, the tiny piece of land, promised to them by God, they will build a new country; here, on this little spot of earth, they will build the Third Temple that will spread light to the entire world, sparkling brightly and by that, eliminating the atrocities of war and evil.

Sarah truly believed that one day, when they finished their hard work and built the country, a miracle would happen and the Messiah would come; the dead ones killed brutally would come to life and she'd meet her sisters, parents, and grandparents again. She felt that they were fulfilling the unique and special mission not just for themselves but for all the nations in the world too.

All her life Sarah took part in drudgery jobs: built the roads, cleaned the houses, silently carrying her burden, and didn't ask questions and like everybody just worked hard hoping for the best future.

In 1948 it finally happened: the country, surrounded by enemies, was founded. The Jewish state which was surrounded by the Arab population, didn't have any chance to survive but it did. Israel got its Independence and was acknowledged by the United Nations. It was not a tale anymore, it was a reality, coming true.

Decades later, whole cities emerged on the map of Israel, the infrastructure grew, and the population increased rapidly; driven by some mysterious power a modern Israel appeared on the map. Jews from all over the world immigrated to Israel and could openly celebrate Jewish holidays and follow Jewish traditions. They were not chased anymore, they were the new Israelis, a strong nation ready to fight for their country and freedom.

Sarah got married and started a family, she had a wonderful life on the kibbutz and even felt happy, but secretly she didn't stop dreaming about Messiah. Every day, before going to sleep, she would look out the window and dream about him. Even today, so many years later, in the retirement home, she is still sitting next to the window and waiting. The staff and the nurses have already got used to a weird old lady, waiting for some Messiah, which didn't exist at all as they thought.

"Doesn't he love me?", she would ask Anastasiya, the new nurse in her thirties.

"Sure, he does", Anastasiya would answer pitifully.

"So where is he? Why hasn't he come? I have been waiting patiently all my life and I don't have much time left. I just wanted to see my sisters and parents for the last time, to hug them and say a proper farewell, is it too much to ask for?".

All of a sudden, she shuddered as remembered that a silly argument with her family saved her life. When she came back home, they were all taken and shot by the Nazis, but Sarah managed to escape.

"Tomorrow we are celebrating Hanukkah, the festival of lights. You should be really happy as your family will arrive for a visit. Please, try not to be sad, your grandchildren will come too", said the nurse helping Sarah to go to bed and turning off the lights.

When Sarah's husband died, she decided to move here to have some company. The visit of the kids and the grandchildren made her forget about the pain for some time but didn't bring her comfort. She still cherished the hope of the Messiah's coming and fulfilling her deep desire.

PART II

On the next day, Sarah woke up in a bad mood asking herself the eternal question, "Where was God when six million Jews were sent into the gas chambers? Maybe, people are right and the Messiah is just a product of her imagination", she thought to herself.

The guests have already arrived and gathered in the dining room. The festive feeling filled this dark and lonely place, elderly people in wheelchairs or holding the walkers began to smile. The kids prepared a dance and the audience cheered them happily.

A plump woman brought doughnuts, and the crowd was getting more and more excited. The doughnuts looked delicious and were of different kinds: the simple ones with strawberry jam and the sophisticated ones with vanilla cream, pistachio, Belgian chocolate, or blueberries, everything a person can just dream about.

Sarah recalled the first Hanukkah in Israel, they barely had flour to bake the doughnuts, and even those modest ones, they had to share because there was not enough. However, they were free and thus happy.

They came hungry for bread and worked hard establishing farms and kibbutzim, so they wouldn't have to rely on anyone any longer. There were times when Sarah had to feed her kids with a couple of eggs and some pieces of bread a day. "So many things have changed since then", she thought to herself, they had an abundance of everything but still something was missing, maybe the secret component that holds the country together?

Maybe, the spirit of Zionism and the faith that some unknown supernatural force was standing by their side, no matter what. The generation of today didn't experience all the hardships of war and Sarah herself wanted to protect her kids from any hardships and spoiled them as much as she could. The modern generation wanted to have everything and too fast, she often thought, they were too attached to material values but Sarah kept her thoughts to herself and never shared them with anyone.

It was time to light the candles and to remember the Hanukkah miracle. Sarah's granddaughter, a red-haired girl, started to read the blessing. The rabbi held the shamash and prayed: "Blessed are you, Adonai, our God, King of the Universe, who has provided us with life and sustained us, and brought us to this moment, Amen".

All of a sudden, amidst all those people, Sarah saw Him… the Messiah appeared, and he came to her to tell her that it was not a dream. A huge smile lifted her face and Sarah realized that Messiah was not necessarily a man of flesh and blood; Messiah might be a true connection between all those people who at the moment of happiness and goodness felt they were one, despite everything that separated between them.

The Messiah was the human creation, the spiritual bond between them all and they had to project the light together in order to see it, to connect to the creator. Sarah thought that it was symbolic. He came on Hanukkah so that they could create the same miracle that happened to their ancestors, the Maccabees, when the oil in the jug that was enough for one day, was burning for the whole eight days in the Temple.

The Maccabees managed to overcome their egoistic desires and put their brotherhood in the first place, their unity and faith darkened the fear, the oil burnt in the light of love and brotherhood; the light overcame everything, and the light from the Temple illuminated the world entirely. They found God.

Happy Hanukkah!

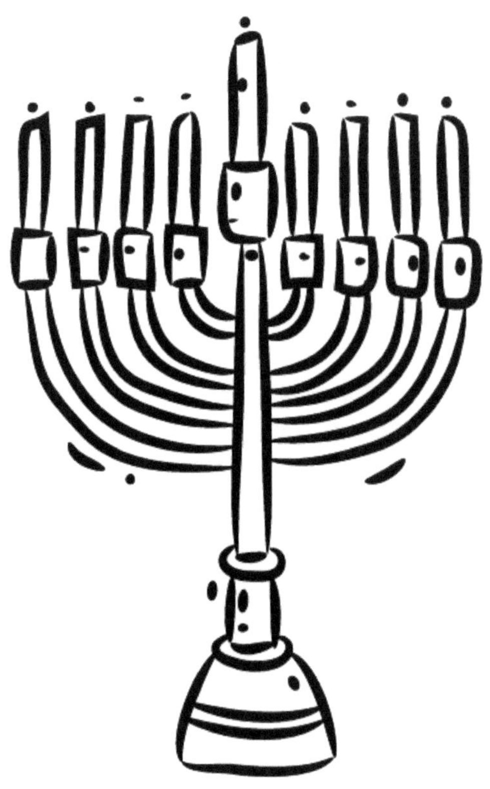

CHAPTER 3

THE LOST PILOTS

1973

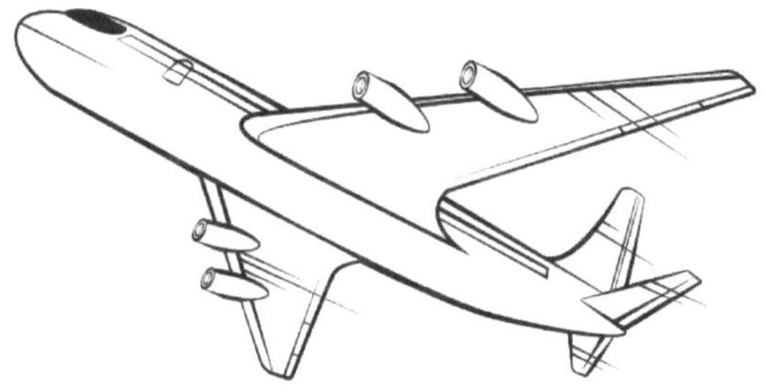

"Would you tell me, please, which way I ought to go from here?
This depends a good deal on where you want to get to.
I don't much care where.
Then it doesn't matter which way you go."

Alice in Wonderland, Lewis Carol

Kobi and Yossi were born Israelis of the first generation parents that survived the Holocaust. Although they never spoke about the atrocities of war, both of them unconsciously knew that they would become pilots when they grew up and would proudly protect their country's borders from its numerous enemies.

Since early childhood, they shared everything, including their lunches in kindergarten and later in school, they shared the same dreams and even fell in love with the same girl, whose name was Alice, a tall blonde girl with blue eyes. Both of them worked hard to fulfill their dreams in the army and to fly the sky of Israel.

Both of them were recruited on the same day and wiped the tears from their mothers' eyes and of Alice's who came to say farewell. They flew together to the sky and felt like superheroes protecting their country from any evil. "If we only had those planes then," said Kobbi once, "we would have bombed those vicious concentration camps in Europe and we might have saved all those Jews, who were murdered just because of their faith".

"But, on the other hand, maybe it was the only way," pointed Yossi high into the sky, "to bring us back home, we can't really know".

They flew above the Mediterranean Sea and Kinneret, over Yehuda desert and Golan Heights, and were always amazed at how this small country was full of natural variety and authentic beauty.

This land kept and could tell so much history from more than 3000 years ago, including the times of Temples and the glorious age of Kings David and Solomon; the era of the Crusades, and King Arthur's knights' quest for a holy grail. No doubt, here was the origin of everything and always will be, it was the indisputable Jewish heritage and always will be.

A day before the Kippur War burst, they sincerely spoke

about Alice and that when they came back home, she'd have to choose between the two of them; but it wouldn't destroy their friendship or brotherhood, nothing but death could separate between them.

Egyptians invaded the sovereign Jewish state unexpectedly and both pilots received an order to attack, for them it was the dream coming true-to protect their people. It was a late and long flight, they had to explode the Egyptian planes. Yossi managed to execute the order but Kobbi's plane disappeared from the radar. The remnants of the plane were never found and he was announced as a missing pilot.

It was a horrible tragedy for Yossi, he was deeply mourning and blaming himself. He lost his brother and felt his one-half was gone, he preferred to be injured physically and not mentally. Alice didn't have to choose, as Yossi was the only one who remained alive; she was always nearby, supporting him in the best way possible.

Years passed and Yossi began to rehabilitate or at least that's what everybody thought. He got married to Alice and went to college. But only he knew that he felt an eternal unbearable pain in his heart, which was constantly bleeding. He felt like he was entering a dark black cloud without a way out. He would walk late at night, suffering from the nightmares and flashbacks of that night when Kobbi was lost. His disease was transparent and nobody could see his heart and soul burning from inside.

During the day, he was suffering from panic attacks and became easily angry and violent, shouting at Alice. On Purim Eve, a gay holiday when it's custom for people to dress in costumes, the kids were exploding the crepitations, (which is part of Israeli tradition), while Yossi was making the salad. When he heard the noise, he felt like returning to the battlefield and entered the state of fight, beginning to attack Alice with the cooking knife.

Some seconds later, he realized that he had almost killed his wife, fell on the floor, and burst into tears like a little child. He was suffering from PTSD but was too afraid to admit it. For him, it was a horrible shame. He hated himself, constantly returning to that cursed day when Kobbi probably crashed and was missing. He felt that he had gone missing too and blamed himself for staying alive; he felt that his life was pointless and miserable.

Two years later, Yossi came back from the soldier's cemetery where he met Kobbi's parents. Memorial Day and Holocaust Remembrance Day always evoke mixed emotions inside his soul-one day to remember all the soldiers that sacrificed their lives for this country and another-to remember the most cruel history of the extermination of Jews. He was so mad with God that he often asked him why it was never enough. When would he stop taking his people's lives? Maybe if Yossi gave his, that would be the end of it?

Yossi never got the answers, he just felt useless in this world. He didn't have any right to existence, or the place. The thoughts captured his mind and he didn't have the powers to resist them anymore. He just wanted to die. Death seemed such a good solution to finish all that suffering.

He began to think what would be the best way to do it quickly and silently when Alice woke up and asked him to bring her a glass of water. She was nine months pregnant. All of a sudden, Yossi realized that it was not fair: an alive woman with his baby inside lying in front and that he didn't really want to commit the most horrible sin-to take his own life.

Yosi felt helpless and began to cry, but Alice immediately realized what he wanted to do and showed compassion.

"You need help, dear, there is nothing to be ashamed of, it can happen to anyone but only the strong ones can ask for help. Asking for help is not a weakness, it's a strength because it means you want to fight. Men are allowed to cry at night too. Tomorrow we'll go to therapy together".

Five years after the Yom Kippur War, on the Eve of the Day

of Judgement, Yossi came to the therapist and took his place in front of a clinical psychologist. This moment symbolized the biggest victory that Yosi has ever experienced in his life-the victory over himself. Yossi opened his heart and began to tell his story from the very start, a story about two missing pilots-one missing in death and the other-missing in life. The more he told it, the more he felt like peeling the shells from the depths of his soul, gaining back his new life with Alice and their child.

The Verdict given is Good Life!

Chapter 4

The Exodus via the Red Sea

It was a stunning spring day in the early spring of 1936. Nature was blooming, the cherry trees began to blossom, the colorful tulips just opened and the smell of the apple trees filled the fresh air. The Rozentzvat family as usual gathered in the yard of their house to celebrate the traditional Passover holiday.

In Poland they were a prosperous and respected family that everybody knew, a grandfather was an engineer in chief. His wife worked as a secretary in his office. The father of the family was an architect and the mother worked as a doctor in a local hospital. There was also a 94-year-old great-grandfather, who was a chief rabbi of the Jewish community in Krakov, and two teenagers, Tzila and Itzik.

Jewish Passover was the major holiday of the year for them but they couldn't celebrate it openly because of the growing wave of antisemitism; nobody spoke about it freely but it was in the air and they could read hatred and anger in the jealous eyes of their neighbors. Glances can sometimes speak better than thousands of unsaid words for those who wish to see them.

Every year they read the traditional Haggadah about the Exodus of their ancestors from Egypt, the story of their nation's exile from Egyptian slavery, and walking in the desert for 40 long years. During the celebration, the Rozentzvat ate traditional Jewish food like chicken soup, gefilte fish, an egg, lettuce, a potato, and of course, the Matza, which substituted for bread during the exile as the regular bread wouldn't rise.

They always kept a bottle of wine for this special occasion, so that everyone could drink four cups to commemorate their freedom. Tzadok, the great grandfather started to read the Passover tale when all of a sudden, he toasted happily: "Next year in Jerusalem!" Everybody looked at each other, thinking that grandpa was probably confused, but as he tried to continue his sentence, he fell and lost consciousness. It was a heart attack.

They called an ambulance and tried to revive him but it was useless. Tzadok passed away. Thousands of people came to the funeral and some even said that it was a blessing of the righteous men to pass on this holy night, reading the prayer. But only Tzila and Itzik remembered that grandpa didn't say any prayer. Actually, he passed away with a Zionist toast frozen on his lips.

The teens couldn't calm down, they were confident that grandpa wanted to tell them something else. He was a wise man and couldn't make such a mistake coincidentally. He wanted to warn them against some casualty or danger as Jews began to feel sort of discrimination and many of them even tried to hide their true identity. The tension and memories of pogroms in Western Europe and Russia were in the air again.

Many families left or disappeared at night feeling the danger coming closer and closer. Some of them even secretly left for Zion or, at least, that's what the rumors said. The teens were always attentively listening to Tzadok's stories about the Jewish heart, longing for Jerusalem, the eternal city; about their secret mission to build the spiritual home for all nations.

There, in the land of "milk and honey", in the middle of nowhere, the huge heart of humankind is beating constantly. Jerusalem, the heart of the universe, can never be destroyed and it's the Jews' mission to return its dimmed light to the world. Jerusalem is located in the grain of the spiritual center and the Temple, rebuilt there, should reflect the light coming from the upward, this light would shine to the world entirely.

Tzila and Itzik spoke to their parents, sharing their fears and thoughts but the adults couldn't understand what was bothering them. "Probably it's their silly age", they decided.

Nonetheless, they promised to go to the synagogue and talk to the rabbi. The rabbi just waved his hand and said: "Nonsense, our community is the strongest now ever since, Jews are doctors, architects, and even members of the court. We are very influential, the government appreciates and nobody will hurt us".

The parents calmed down that it was an exaggeration of the teen's age and nothing more. They couldn't leave anyway, they had property, jobs, respect, and so forth. They couldn't leave all that just for nothing, not for some doubtful freedom.

However, Tsila and Itzik didn't calm down, they were sure that a tragedy was on its way that it was only a matter of time, and that they could lose more than their material possessions. They decided to run away together, alone. If the parents weren't listening, they would leave Krakov for good by themselves. Next year, they will be celebrating Passover in Jerusalem, that was the plan.

A night before an escape, they were planning silently all the details, Itzik was drawing a map, explaining to Tzila: "Tomorrow at nine o'clock, when everybody leaves the house, we'll take a train to the port. There is a boat that is sailing to Palestine. I've got the tickets and bribed one of the sailors to let us in. The voyage will last for three weeks, so make sure we've got enough cans for this time. The most dangerous spot is here," pointed Itzik to the map, which meant nothing to Tzila, and continued. "The British soldiers are drowning the boats with Jewish immigrants, but don't worry, we'll hold each other and pray as grandpa taught us: 'Hear O Israel the Lord Our God, God is One'", finished Itzik.

Only God alone knew where exactly the boat would dock in the Mediterranean. Itzik assumed that somewhere near the Suez Canal, they would then arrive at the Sinai Peninsula and travel ten kilometers by foot in the desert, endangering their lives again as there are many wild animals and snakes. Then the grandpa's friend would meet them and take them to Tzfat, a hometown of many kabbalists, which would bring them luck too.

Tzila kept quiet. She was scared and sunk in her thoughts, 'What if... what if they don't survive? What if they don't see their family again? What if the idea is insane?

"Do you realize that we won't forgive ourselves if something happens to them?", she finally asked.

"Do you remember that grandpa told us about free will, the one that makes us like a creator and closer to Adonai? You cannot force anyone to do something against his will and should respect the choice. You can still stay home if you decide", said Itzik. Tzila doubted no more.

The next day they set out on a journey, taking the most necessary things only. They had each other and that's what mattered. They got up on the boat and sailed for three weeks, hugging and praying on the stormy nights. They did not have much food, were hungry and thirsty and a frail hope was the only thing that kept them alive.

Finally, they arrived in the Sinai Desert and were about to enter Palestine, the land promised to them by God. Their legs were injured and scratched, Tzila couldn't feel her lips and arms, and Itzik suffered from an ulcer. All that didn't matter at all. When Tzila looked at the Eilat Mountains and the Red Sea, which her people crossed fleeing from the huge Egyptian army, she couldn't believe that they made it. It was a pure living miracle.

When Tzila looked at the promised land, she realized that maybe there was not a Pharaoh or even slavery. Maybe, the Haggadah was a story about going out of the prison of one's ego that remained there, in a far away Poland, in a slavery. Itzik and Tzila were the only ones in the Rosentzvat family who managed to set free from their inner slavery. They reached the Red Sea and two years later, the pogroms "Kristallnacht" swept Europe, they did not meet their family ever again.

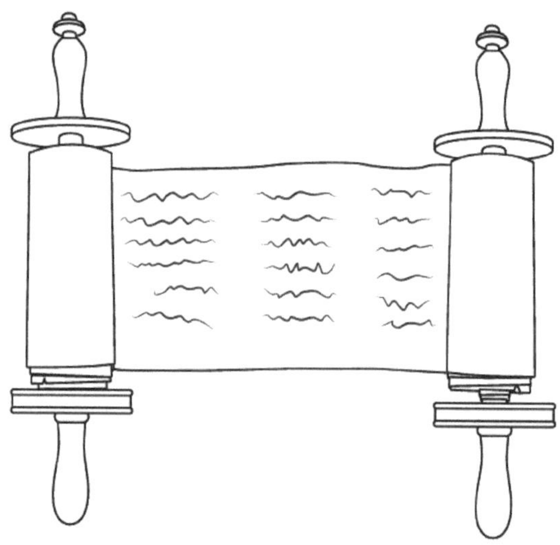

CHAPTER 5

An Apple in Honey

Who could believe that in 2020 people would wear masks and gloves, stay at home, and stop meeting each other? Who could imagine that the world Pandemic would close them at homes and modern medicine would prove useless just like in ancient times? Liya could not imagine that a few days before the Jewish New Year, her business would be paralyzed while the phone wouldn't stop ringing during that time all the other years.

Unfortunately, that was the reality, proving that people were not in charge of their fortunes and that some upper force was ruling from above and planning their schedules. Liya thought that nature stopped them on purpose from their every day, often useless chores to make them look inside and reflect on their lives. It looked like there was so simply no other way.

"The prophecy has begun to come true", thought Liya to herself, "we are the last generation, the ego reached its final stages of development, and all the masks are taken off. Hatred is overflowing everywhere, our nation is torn apart from the inside, the country is bleeding, and we are speaking the same language, but do not understand each other. We are arguing about vanity, secular and religious, right and left, Ethiopians, Russians, and Moroccans, no wonder that catastrophes are happening. What future awaits us?"

Liya didn't want to believe it was the end of it, after Moses led them for 40 years in the desert, they survived the Holocaust and returned to their homeland and all that was in vain. She couldn't believe that they were giving up on the most precious gift, their country, that got so easily. They had an abundance of everything in the land of endless resources and still, they felt an emptiness that was so difficult to satisfy since the desires and the ambitions grew up. They got lost in a desert and could not find the well that would fill them in.

Liya was also worried about the future of humankind, so many people were infected or died; nobody could predict how long the Pandemic would last and there was no proper treatment. In addition to that, Liya was worried that so many people would be left without her beautiful flowers, making the holiday especially miserable for lonely or elderly people. She felt again that they were just the puppets in the show of an incredibly talented producer.

The next day Liya decided to go to the plant nursery and try to do at least something. "The Flowers Village" was a home for many special people who were autistic or had other disabilities. They were mature but naive just like the kids and that was their authentic beauty.

"We should learn from them, they are innocent and pure souls coming into the world to make us better," she thought to herself as one of the women asked her if she wanted to be her friend.

"Of course," answered Liya as her eyes filled with tears, and promised to visit again. They helped to collect the flowers, giving enthusiastic explanations about each of them and Liya thought that it was unbelievable there is life behind the fence that the outer world might not be even aware of. She hugged them despite the prohibition, thinking that even corona can't forbid being human.

On Rosh Hashanah Eve, Liya wrote a message on Facebook asking volunteers to come and help her distribute the flowers and seedlings. She did not expect that so many people would show up. She also did not expect that other people would think about the same idea. The volunteers were distributing the flowers, food and even the blankets making sure that nobody was left without a sweet taste of an apple dipped in honey, a Jewish tradition for wishing a happy year.

When Liya looked around, she could not believe that people were not scared to leave their houses in the middle of the Pandemic. Kindness was contagious. They were the "last generation" that would rise above everything and put aside all the conflicts for the common good and prosperity. They will build the spiritual home of pulsating hearts for all religions, thus materializing their deeply embedded spirituality. Just like the man who traveled in the desert ages ago with his friends and suddenly found a well, they, the new Israelis, will blow in the shofar to make sure their comrades can hear the loud noise that will awaken them and show them the right way.

Part Two

The Angel

CHAPTER 6

AMY

Amy took off her clothes and fell on the bed, she was exhausted, it was such a long day that she just wanted nothing. She could not get why the photographer insisted on changing the lighting or decorations, they would do photoshop anyway and nobody would see Amy, a beautiful young woman coming to conquer Paris a year ago from Israel.

Every morning Amy spent in a cozy coffee shop next to her little apartment in downtown Paris, ordering traditional coffee and croissant. She even befriended the owner of the bakery Muhamad, who originally came from the same geographical zone-The Middle East. But the taste of the croissant became worse and worse from day to day, thought Amy to herself, it contained the same ingredients but tasted differently. She didn't feel the same excitement she felt during the first days of her visit to the city of lights and fashion.

She had already used to be in the center of a spotlight and knew that she could get any man she wanted. It flattered her in the beginning when the most influential men were at her feet and sent her expensive presents just for an opportunity to share her company for one evening. But fame fades just like the flowers and the attention didn't thrill her anymore. Moreover, she always remained faithful to the same man, who was her producer and her first lover.

Of course, she had intimacy with other men too, but for her, it was pure business and didn't matter. Amy knew that she could use her natural beauty to get what she wanted but it filled her just for a limited time. She realized that to become a successful model, she had to adopt the same code of behavior as other models did. Modeling was dirty business and the girls often had to escort the clients after the shows. Everybody knew that and tried to turn a blind eye. "All that is gold does not glitter", said Shakespeare and Amy adopted the idea.

The models worked extremely hard, often staying for the extra hours at night, didn't eat properly, and couldn't lead a normal way of life. Furthermore, the competition was so tense that they used deceitful methods to promote, amid which spending a night with a producer or designer was considered legitimate. Amy also had to do the same thing and that's actually how she came to Paris.

Eventually, Amy reached her goal and was on a pedestal, she became a famous supermodel, earning millions a year, but the price she had to pay was too high. She felt her psychic was hurt forever and she secretly went to a physiatrist, trying to silence her pain with psychiatric drugs. She knew it was just a plaster, and that the injury would bleed again, but, at least, it temporarily helped and helped her fall asleep.

Amy was born in northern Tel Aviv, her parents were artists relating themselves to Bohemian society. Her mom was a designer, and her dad was a barber, who owned a small business of his own. Amy was the only daughter and felt the burden of her parents' expectations lying heavily on her shoulders.

She was the best student in school and immediately was accepted into the University. She went to celebrate her school graduation in the company of friends in one of Tel Aviv's pubs when a famous producer paid attention to a tall and slim blond girl with blue eyes. She looked totally like Barbie in the pink dress she wore on the same day.

Meir, the producer and photographer, knew that she was an excellent and authentic "product" that would be sold well in the market. He advised her to enter the business and was always by her side, recommending her the best deals. Amy felt appreciated for being herself for the first time in her life and easily fell in love with Meir and there she was sharing the bed with her producer, blurring the boundaries between personal and professional.

That night Amy was looking out of the window of her penthouse on the 25th floor, seeing Paris in all its beauty: the Eiffel Tower and Arc de Triomphe, the lights of the city were not making her happy or satisfied. She wore a white bath robe and drank the fanciest champagne with strawberries but it didn't please her either, she would switch places with any other regular girl.

She had already called Meir a hundred times, leaving him messages and asking him to call her back: "Meir I feel really bad, please, call me back. I need you". There was no answer, Meir was already busy looking for another model as the time of stars passes quickly and everybody forgets them very soon.

Amy filled her glass again, then took the psychiatric pill and then another one… and one more glass of champagne: "L'chaim!" to life, said Amy to herself and finished the whole bottle of champagne. She thought that those pills helped her sleep and that if she took the whole package, she would fall asleep forever. That's what she wanted since only in her dreams could she feel alive. And so she did, swallowing the whole package of pills, in the center of a luxurious apartment in the center of Paris.

A housekeeper named Suzi found Amy in the morning when as usual she came to wake her up for a coffee with croissant. Amy was barely breathing, and Suzy immediately called the ambulance that took Amy to one of the hospitals in the center of the city. Glory does not always shine brightly, thought a cleaning lady to herself.

Anna

Anna Karenina, Leo Tolstoy

Anna was standing on the cliff and looking at the stormy and dark sea, which reflected her mental state -the darkest day of her life. All her dreams were smashed into different little pieces at once, her life was destroyed and there was no point in staying alive. She still tried to keep breathing somehow but got carried away and couldn't keep herself above the giant waves of the water, drowning deeply inside her thoughts. She had already wanted to jump when she heard the voice of a stranger, telling her softly: "The sea is really cold today, let's go for a swim tomorrow."

Anna was so surprised that unintentionally moved around and saw a strange man. She couldn't tell if it was a coincidence or if he understood her true intentions. The man offered her his hand gently and she climbed down. He was an angel, coming from the sky, Anna thought later, who came to save her from the most horrible mistake she was going to make.

"My name is Abraham, but you can call me Avi," the man introduced himself. "I live nearby, and we can drink hot chocolate together, then I'll take you home if you want".

Anna was shaking from cold, and anxiety and he sounded so natural and sincere that Anna believed him and gave him her hand. They walked slowly together, two strangers that became close in one moment.

They were drinking hot chocolate and Avi covered her with a warm blanket, then Anna began to tell her story. She was the most successful law student in the course, which was not surprising. She grew up in a family of generational lawyers, judges, and attorneys, making this choice of profession inevitable. From a young age, she listened to her parents solving the crimes and building the defense strategy.

Anna didn't have any problem entering the faculty and everybody predicted her the best future possible, she was smart and intelligent. She had already begun law practice during the third year of her studies, where she met David, her future husband, a successful and nice-looking lawyer in his thirties.

It was love at first sight, at least that's what Anna thought in the beginning. On the first date, Anna stayed in David's house for a whole night, he served her breakfast in bed and it seemed like a dream coming true. A month later, Anna was already pregnant and found herself marrying the man of her dreams.

Anna graduated from university with excellence, nursing a baby on her hands and discovering being pregnant with another. Obviously, she had to leave the practice.

"How ironic!", she thought later. She became a family attorney, and she could not manage her own family. It would be impossible to combine two kids and her career, David thought.

"Why do you need to work at all? I have an office of my own and earn enough money, you'll stay at home and raise our kids. I want you to be calm and relaxed when I come home after a difficult day. You will take care of me and spoil us," summarized David without really giving her any choice.

His arguments sounded so logical and convincing that they didn't leave space for a dispute. However, deep inside she felt hurt like someone put out her inner sparkle, devaluing her. She thought it was unfair that a woman with the same education as a man would stay at home taking care of the family and suppressing her inner passion. But she thought he was right and said nothing, hoping at least to help him with challenging cases at home.

Anna was unwell through her second pregnancy, she felt mentally and physically toxic. Once she even tried to talk to David about it, but he said she was exaggerating.

"Why should you be sad, you've got everything a normal woman could simply dream about, it's probably the hormones and will soon be over".

She began to feel even worse, being ashamed of her emotions, and feeling selfish and useless.

But sadness did not disappear after Anna gave birth; on the contrary: it only increased. Anna felt horrible and could not even look at a newborn baby as it evoked rejection, she felt inner anger and aggression, despising herself. She did not share her feelings with anyone again as she was scared to be blamed and judged, just like David did, just like solicitors did, just like her parents always did.

Years passed and Anna could finally put the kids into the kindergartens, returning to her profession. Unexpectedly, Anna woke up feeling dizzy one day and after taking a pregnancy test, discovered she was pregnant again.

"Oh no," she screamed miserably as she recalled the night David took her out and she forgot to take a pill.

Anna did not want to have more kids, at least not now. She spoke in the evening to David and he only disregarded her: "You cannot abort my kid, I won't allow you. You are staying at home anyway, so you can stay for a couple of years, the court will somehow manage and nothing dramatic will happen".

This time Anna felt smashed, she felt that someone was stealing her fate, and she wanted her life back. She was depressed and wanted to be that courageous and ambitious girl again when she met David. One day she decided to pay a visit to her husband's office. She went to the hairdresser, bought a new dress, and decided to surprise David with a homemade lunch.

She passed through reception, leaving the secretary dazzled and trying to say something to her, opened the door of the office and saw him. She saw her husband naked kissing and touching another woman, at least ten years younger than her. Unexpectedly, she felt a relief: the curtains lifted in front of her eyes, and she saw the whole truth she knew about but was too scared to admit.

David came often late at night claiming that he was working hard to satisfy all of her and the kids' needs. He stopped taking interest in her as a woman and they rarely made love. This girl was probably one of his students just like Anna once was, just like so many others that Anna did not know about.

Anna's perfect life shattered just in front of her eyes, and she didn't know how to deal with it. She could not call her parents either since they were against her marriage from the very start, she asked the babysitter to look after the kids and her legs brought Anna to the seashore.

Chapter 8

Nadav

Nadav was born to a family of a dynasty of doctors: his parents worked the senior doctors in the governmental hospital, his grandpa was a professor of medicine and a lecturer in the University, and they also owned a private clinic of alternative medicine in Even Yehuda. The parents worked very hard all day long and barely spent time with their sons, Nadav and Yakov, his elder brother and a student of medicine.

Yakov was considered a successful brother from all perspectives; he was a student of the medicine faculty and often organized huge parties in their enormous house. He used to bring a lot of friends from the University and the students of medicine could relax from a tense day in the morgue practicing on the dead bodies. They were students from middle-class families who won the lottery ticket into luxury life since their very birth. They felt masters of life and used to do drugs, drank tequila unstoppably, and had random sex every day in the swimming pool or the numerous bedrooms of the house. This way they could forget about the corpses, Yakov used to say.

Nadav saw all that debauchery but kept quiet, being afraid to rat on his brother. He also knew that the parents would never believe him since Yakov was their pride, they had already prepared a place for him in their clinic. Yakov would often bribe his brother by helping him with his school homework, and house chores and asking some drunk girl to amuse him; without paying attention, Nadav became the participant of all this immoral debauchery.

Nadav often had pangs of conscience and felt guilty, but every time he tried to talk to his parents, something stopped him. They were very busy people, having time just for their patients, which was fair, Nadav tried to justify them. The ill people needed them much more than him. Nadav couldn't put himself first and always felt like being brought up in the shadow of his brother.

Yakov was always smarter than him in everything including in studies, the teachers always praised him and the parents adored him. Nadav, on the other hand, was not that brilliant in school. He had ADHD and even stuttered when he got nervous. Nadav's teacher even once called his mom and asked her to come to school and talk about it. But Nadav's mother felt insulted: "We don't have people with a short attention span in our family", was her arrogant answer, like there was something to be ashamed of. Nadav felt he was a defect, a shame on his family, a failure.

One day, when they had a pool party again, the students became too drunk and noisy, so the neighbors called the police. When the police arrived, they were shocked by the mess and naked young people lying on the floor everywhere, they found drugs, alcohol, and condoms in horrible amounts. They also found heroin.

They asked Yakov who it belonged to and the elder brother decided to accuse Nadav, "Nadav was a teenager and wouldn't be pressed with charges but if I went to prison, my career would have been ruined", he said later trying to find excuses. His friends supported that version and Nadav was blamed for the crime he didn't commit. His birth was a crime, he thought to himself at this moment of total injustice.

Nadav began to stutter and could not speak for himself. If Yakov thought it was the only possibility to get out of it, that was probably the right choice. Yakov doesn't make mistakes, he's perfect, that's what everybody used to say since Nadav was a child. So let it be, the world was unfair toward him all his life, so it didn't change anything. Nadav admitted to the crime he did not commit.

The parents weren't surprised at all, Nadav always disappointed their expectations, they paid a ransom to take him home and were looking for a lawyer to take him out. That night Nadav could not fall asleep. He knew where Yakov kept drugs and decided to inject a double dose. Nobody will pay attention to his disappearance anyway; on the contrary, they will be relieved as he will not embarrass them any longer.

He woke up the next morning in the hospital, his soul flying gently over his body, he saw doctors surrounding his body and trying to bring him back to life. He realized what had happened, he experienced a near-to-death state, NDE, just like he saw in the movies. Nonetheless, he wasn't scared at all; on the contrary, he felt at peace with himself and loved like never before. He felt that his spirit was connected to all the souls in the Universe and they loved him unconditionally and unlimitedly. At this moment the angels were touching his soul and the light of creation went through him.

Nobody spoke to him and he didn't see the angels or his dead relatives, but his faith was beyond knowledge, he believed in the things that he didn't see. The information was flowing at the speed of light, "the words were only redundant and disturbing the flow of emotions", he thought. Here, in the upper world, he realized that he didn't commit any crime and that his birth was a blessing and not a curse or a coincidence. There is nothing coincidental in this world and everything aligns with the purpose of the creation. He had to return and teach his family the endless love he experienced right now and even when you are not perfect, you deserve all the love in the world. That was his mission.

CHAPTER 9

ALON

"You should never ask anyone for anything.
Never-and especially from those who are more powerful than
yourself".

Master and Margarita, Michael Bulgakov

Alon functioned as the supreme manager in the Hi-tech company of his own. He built this business with his two hands and was a working horse all his life. He was so proud of himself that ten years after its foundation, his company grew rapidly, transforming a small business into a successful and influential start-up company.

Alon was proud that he followed his dream and took a loan back then, he knew he risked everything including his family's wellness. Luckily, his wife Libi stood always by his side, supporting him in all his innovations, and taking care of the family. Alon's only baby was his company and he cautiously chose his workers, setting a high standard and expecting the same from the staff. Those who failed to meet his expectations were immediately fired without any further explanation. Business, nothing more.

If the employee approached him asking for extra time to finish the project and explaining the excuses, Alon had a standard answer: "Everybody has a family or gets sick, that's the standard and we should be the best in our sphere. We can't even miss a day, our competitors will beat us. Business is a harsh game, the goodness of the company is the highest priority".

"The highest priority". How ironic Alon thought now, looking back and recalling his sentences. At this time, when he was lying in bed terminally sick and out of control of his life, he thought about how much time he just wasted chasing the abundance. What if he could go back in time, he would have lived a different life, spending more time with his kids and Libi, prioritizing other values.

After Passover, Alon began to feel unwell, but of course never paid attention to his health, persuading himself that it was a temporary fatigue and would be over soon. When the pains in the stomach increased, he blamed his diet and never approached the doctor, putting the company first and not having time for himself. Nevertheless, the ache increased over time, disturbing his night's sleep. On the Shavuot holiday, the feast festival, he had a fever and started to spit blood. He was throwing out the food and couldn't fight with his body anymore. It definitely had a message for him, it was telling him something he tried to ignore for so long.

When Libi brought Alon to the emergency room in Beilinson Hospital, the doctors took him to the check-ups and a gray-haired elderly doctor came out with the result.

"We are sorry to inform you that you have got colorectal cancer, stage 3. We can't tell if you have got metastases till the operation. We will talk about the next stage and the chemotherapy only after the surgery". The doctor finished and left.

For him, it was just an everyday job, just like for Alon was his business. Alon was left shocked and lost. How the hell could all that have happened to him? Is it some kind of a joke? He was healthy like a bull all his life.

"It's definitely a mistake", was the only phrase he said to Libi who as usual was there.

Libi could see the agony in his eyes and, although she knew it was not a mistake and that was too much for Alon to admit, she agreed to visit another, private hospital with him.

Unfortunately, the private clinic verified the original diagnosis and advised Alon to go to the surgery in a couple of days before it was too late to save his life. It was unbelievable! He was only 50 years old, a manager of a large company, the kids grew up and he could finally start living. How could life have played such a cruel joke? Alon could not handle the situation.

"We will survive. Maybe it's a sign from above that you need to take a break", said humbly Libi holding gently his arm.

She was so calm and touching that Alon could not understand how he hadn't seen this previously in his life. She was the only one who really cared about him.

He began to recall all those numerous employees who were treated unfairly by him, realizing that he detached himself emotionally from them, never taking any interest in their lives. He just wanted somehow to improve the situation or apologize for making them feel bad. He felt that God was punishing him for being so mean and indifferent to other people.

A few days later, Alon underwent a complicated surgery that lasted for hours. When he was in recovery in his hospital room, the same doctor entered the room to deliver the news. "Unluckily, the situation is much worse than we thought: you've got metastases. Some of them were in the lungs which were impossible to reach. We will start with chemo right away in the morning, hoping that the violent treatment will reach those damaged cells."

It was a nightmare materializing in his reality. Alon could not even digest the doctor's words, nor apply them to himself. "Libi, I don't want to die, please, I missed so many real things in my life", was crying this big strong man and the whole clinic could hear this scream.

"You aren't dying", said Libi compassionately and added, "You'll see after you recover, we'll even travel to Thailand like you have been dreaming about since our honeymoon", said Libi resiliently, making Alon believe that there still was hope. Libi also took care of the company, making sure it continued to function even while her husband was missing.

His faithful secretary called him one day and told him that they all were missing him and wished him a quick recovery. When Alon finished the conversation, he felt even worse. He was such a jerk, he did not pay attention to all those people; for him, there were just pawns in his chess game. He did not care about them at all, sometimes even forgetting their names.

He felt like it was his Judgement Day when he could finally reflect on his behavior and admit his mistakes. He had so much free time now like never before, he recalled all the times when he insulted his employees intentionally or without meaning bad, about the times he fired the most loyal of them.

He even remembered a case when one of his workers got cancer and underwent treatment, he was forgetful and exhausted. Alon suggested to him to take respectful compensation and rest till he recovered, justifying his behavior with good intentions, and silencing his ego. It seemed that the boomerang had found its way back to him; he was in the worker's shoes. It didn't make him feel any better, he realized that the only thing a sick person needed was empathy and compassion. He was blind and did not see or appreciate the human abundance he had.

A month later a doctor told him that the chemo did not give the desired results, and they should increase the dosage.

"Do whatever you want," answered Alon, "I don't want to live like that anyway".

The doctor frowned. He saw so many terminated patients and knew that the only way to defeat the disease depended on the patient's will. He saw miracles happening and the patients who had no chance recovered. Being a doctor and a scientist, he could not logically explain that; when the divine force came for help, the impossible became possible. But it was up to the patient to decide whether he wanted to fight.

Two months later, after Alon underwent 50 chemo sessions, he lost 20 kilos and was bald and pale. He could barely walk, eat or talk. During one of the visits, when Libi brought him a bouquet of white lilies, a symbol of hope, and chocolates from his colleagues, Alon felt they were so much better than him. He told Libi, "Please help me to end all this, I don't want to suffer anymore, I don't want to live like that".

But Libi concealed her emotions and answered with undoubtful resilience.

"Dear Alon, it's not just your body that is suffering, it's also your spirit. You are undergoing severe depression, it's when the soul and mind die before the body does. I had it once, I know exactly how it feels. Tomorrow I will call the doctor that I know well, he will help you", said Libi and left, sustaining Alon puzzled again since he couldn't recall Libi ever being depressed.

CHAPTER 10

THE ANGEL

On the morning of the amazing autumn day of the Sukkot holiday, when the leaves began to fall and colored red, yellow, and orange, they gathered in Succa, special huts that Jews built in the desert during their exile from Egypt. They were so different and had so much in common: Anna, Amy, Nadav, and Alon, the broken hearts aspiring to connect. They did not gather to celebrate the holiday or their freedom from slavery, they gathered here for group therapy, and it was symbolic. It symbolized a new beginning, redemption, and hope to find comfort and meaning.

They came from totally different socio-economic statuses and probably wouldn't meet anywhere in the real world, but as we already said, God works in mysterious ways. A successful young supermodel, an attorney in her thirties who became a housewife, a middle-class teenager, and a boss of a startup company in his fifties.

The white Succa was festively and colorfully decorated with lanterns, plants, and other decorations, making this moment unique and special. A cute nurse in a white robe brought a kettle with coffee, milk, cups, and an apple pie. She knew that the therapy would last long hours, and it took time for the patients to start talking.

A nice-looking doctor in his sixties wearing glasses and walking slowly, entered the place. He didn't threaten his patients with ET, he neither tied them to the chairs nor shouted at them as many people are prejudiced against the therapists. He introduced himself smiling and observing them. Yuri worked as a psychiatrist and also had a specialty in clinic psychology for almost thirty years. He looked straight at the patient's soul that kept so many scars and secrets, that could tell a whole life story.

He could not understand why the most important part of the human body and essence of human existence was so neglected, people always turned to treatment when their arms or legs hurt, but they rarely came to treat their wounds unless it was almost too late. Yuri thought that our mind was the most unique organ, it made us, the authentic human being. Through all his long practice, he could not recall two similar souls, even twins had different ones. That was the authentic beauty that our spirit possessed alone.

All of the patients kept quiet, he knew that he should give them time. He also knew that at some point they would start talking as it always happened. It was human nature; surviving was the major instinct. Yuri was born into a communist regime where everything was concealed or forbidden and had to reveal the truth by himself, which he finally did. He also experienced a crisis at some point, constantly looking for the true meaning of everything.

Where do we come from and where do we go? What makes us laugh and cry, fall in love, hate, morn or get angry and insulted? These were the questions that fascinated him.

He constantly was looking for the answers to all those questions and that was what led him to become a doctor of the human soul. He saw patients in horrible conditions, coming back to life, fighting for their lives, and finding their true self. Some of them managed to gain their life back, and some gave up, but most of them saw the illusions imposed by society and realized that they didn't want to be led anymore. Many of the patients perceived that they were the most important person in their lives and that they had the right to live a life of their own, according to their highest purpose.

"Life's a stage and men and women are merely actors", broke the silence Amy, surprising everyone with her knowledge of the eternal classics. "One day you are on top of the world and all men are at your feet. The next day you are at the bottom of it with the same miserable people like you," she finished.

"At least you were lucky to taste fame and be successful", continued Anna sharing her thoughts. "I became a housewife with a high education and future of the first-class attorney. I sacrificed everything for my narcissistic husband and even helped him with his work, he never gave me credit, of course", she laughed sadly. "Eventually he cheated on me with his intern, the same age I was when we got married. She simply came and stole everything from me, how deceitful!"

"At least your kids had you! I felt like an orphan with the living parents. They never had time, nor space for me, were always busy with their patients, friends, conferences, clinic, or my brother," exclaimed Nadav.

The conversation began to flow just like Yurii expected.

"But my workers were always there for me, even late at night, that was me who didn't appreciate them and couldn't see beyond his immediate objectives," intervened Alon. "I didn't see people behind them, didn't care about their private lives, families of feelings", he summed up.

Yuri looked happy, he was satisfied that the patients began to talk, they managed to find the uniting thread between them that should lead them finally out of depression. He added: "I have been looking for the meaning in life since I was a child. I remember myself looking at the tops of the trees, the horizon, or the sunrise and asking what stands beyond all that. Who created that and what comes next?"

The patients looked amazed; they were curious to know the answer. "I read any literary piece I could find in the Soviet Union, it was hard. But when you aspire so much, you can always find it. I was desperately reading all the articles, books, and journals I could find in a dictatorship that promised us a bright future. Soon enough I realized it was a Utopia that would never happen no matter how badly people believed in propaganda that was interested in human robots."

"I realized that the only man who could make this future happen was myself, that is why I always doubted and never believed what others said till I figured out the truth by myself. That's how I found meaning. Actually, I find it everywhere: in my practice, in this clinic, in this Succa sitting with you".

The patients were touched by Yuri's story.

"I still can't see the meaning of everything that happened to me. I wanted to be famous but, finally, fame almost killed me, I felt emptiness each time I succeeded", reflected Amy.

"I felt that every child was taking part of me and that was swallowing me from the inside. I felt like losing myself and living the life of someone else, I even asked myself if that hopeless woman who looked at me in the mirror was actually me", shared Anna.

"I just wanted my parents to see and love me for myself and not for my talents. I never wanted to be a doctor, it was their choice, not mine", said Nadav.

"I just wanted to be efficient and look what happened to me in the end", exclaimed Alon in despair.

The expression of emotions was a good sign, it meant that

the patients wanted to fight for their lives. Sometimes the answers lay on the surface and he had to help them see what was so obvious.

"Nadav, did you inject heroin because you felt it was the only way you could get your parents' attention?" asked Yuri.

Yuri targeted right and Nadav burst into tears like a small child.

"I feel exactly the same", said Amy. "The only way to draw my parents' attention was by becoming famous, but glory did not make me happy at all. When I was a model, I felt like a statue in a museum that had to please everyone with its beauty. It's unfair! I deserve to be loved with all my imperfections, even when I take off my expensive clothes and makeup, I deserve simply to be Amy!" finished Amy dramatically.

"And I deserve to build my career even if I'm a mother, I have a right to decide how many kids and when I want and I'm allowed to talk about my feelings without being judged!", said Anna and added that her husband is also suing her for being a bad mother.

Everybody was shocked and sympathized with Anna.

"Human connection as always could heal the world", the doctor thought.

Yuri was sitting quietly and observing them all. He knew that today they set a beginning to a new life and, although the way was still long, he believed in his patients, he believed that time and effort would heal. The more these people would talk sincerely, the more their hearts would open to each other. He also kept a small secret to himself since he knew that there was someone else, invisible, in this beautiful Succa. He knew that the creator himself was present here and that the patients created him by themselves, inducing the strongest spiritual powers and the upper force that they discovered in themselves at the moment they opened their hearts to others.

Open your heart and let the light in!

PART THREE

THE HEROES

CHAPTER 11

THE HEROES

Thousands of years ago in the Babylon Kingdom around the time of the destruction of Babylon Tower, there lived a brave man named Abraham. He couldn't accomplish a horrible situation of the rise of ego and people hating each other and arguing over vanity. He turned to the creator, the one and the only God of his fathers and grandfathers. He asked him to repair his human desire and that raised above the desires of others.

His sincere prayer, from the bottom of his heart, pleased the creator deeply and he decided to fulfill it. An angel appeared and announced that Abraham and the people that would follow him would become His people, the chosen people, the ones whose mission would be to repair humanity and to return dimmed light to the world. Their path will be full of challenges and deadly obstacles and tests, they will suffer a lot and will even be persecuted. But they should always keep faith in their God and know that he'll find a way to reach them and bring them salvation; even from the ashes, they will be reborn again.

He will stretch his Almighty hand even in the total darkness and will lead them to light. Eventually, after standing strong and courageous against all the odds and countless enemies, they will become "Light unto the Nations". All other nations will follow them because they will see the unnatural miracles happening to them and realize the power of the creator, the one and only God of the whole Universe, the Lord of Abraham, Itzhak, and Yaakov.

On Saturday morning of a bright sunny Jewish holiday–Simchat Torah, the book delivered to Moses on Sinai Mount after his exile from Egypt, fifty years after the Yom Kippur War, cruel inhuman monsters invaded the sovereign country of Israel. They did not want land or peace, their only aim was to massacre as many Jews as possible, just like the Nazis did during the Holocaust. They murdered barbarically young women and little girls, raping, flouting, and humiliating them first. They burned innocent babies in their beds, opened belies of the pregnant women with hexes, and conducted medieval penalties, dismembering peoples' bodies into little pieces.

On the morning of October 7th, 2023, thousands of Hamas terrorists invaded our cities and kibbutzim, reversing Heaven into Hell, exploding the fence, turning off the communication and abusing the innocent civilians right in their homes, stabbing, burning and taking them hostages. They ambushed and jammed the roads and the IDF could not arrive for a long time, leaving almost disarmed civilians to struggle for many hours alone. The terrorists thought that it was the end of us, but they were so wrong.

One cannot eliminate the eternal just like it is impossible to exterminate Jews and faith, no matter how hard many nations have tried to find "the final solution" through our tragic history. We are and always will be since we are channeling the upper force, containing the divine light and thus protected by it. Israel, straight to the Lord, will stand forever; Jerusalem the eternal city, will survive any destruction and even ruined, will be rebuilt again. That's why despite all the atrocities, unbearable pain, and horrible destruction, the Jewish nation still prevails. Our courageous soldiers, the army of Lions, protect us from the strongest armies of enemies, our God stands by us in the darkest moments never breaking the indisputable spiritual alliance He made with Abraham.

Our enemies managed to kill our bodies and pull our hearts away, but they will never kill our spirit because it is connected to the essence of the very source, to the very heart of creation. Jews were chosen to carry the highest right and responsibility - to spread light to the nations worldwide and to heal the world. Thus, we will prevail no matter what till we complete our mission, till we spread the divine light on Earth.

The victims of this inhuman horrible tragedy paid with their lives and we will always remember them, just as we will remember all the soldiers falling for this country and the victims slaughtered in the name of the false Jihad. True Islam just like Judaism, promotes the laws and morality of God and comes from the same source. We will also remember all the Jews slaughtered in the name of heresy, inquisition, and antisemitism.

We will recall again what a nation of heroes we are: the fighters of Judah, the descendants of the Maccabees, the martyrs arising from the ashes of Nazi machines. We will mourn together over the lives of our brothers, taken brutally before their time, look at the sky in Israel, so close to God, and there are the endless stars of David, the stars of their lives.

Am Israel Chai! Long live Israel!

CHAPTER 12

THE LATE CORPORAL "R"

On the third day of the war for its existence, 75 years after regaining its Independence and after 2000 years of exile, the soldiers who were fighting bravely till their last drop of blood were brought to burial. Among them was a young corporal "R".

He had just graduated from high school, was an excellent student, and might have a bright future ahead of him, but his life was abruptly taken when the war burst. He was one of the first soldiers who came to rescue the civilians. He gave his life saving the others, never fulfilling his dreams.

The cemetery was crowded with people, everyone came to say farewell asking himself if he deserved that sacrifice. That was the most powerful and emotional experience, breaking the heart into little pieces and stitching it together in the national grief. It was a horrible loss for everybody; anybody there felt like he lost his son. We were mourning and crying together, stranding our teeth and giving a supportive shoulder.

The Lord accepted his son in his generous arms and "R" felt at peace coming home, but he also felt anger, "R" was angry with those who stayed here for letting it happen. Looking from above, he asked us not to sin again and to stand stronger and united than ever before in the face of the collective threat, even if the whole world stood against us.

And out of the broken heart, we realized that this tragedy didn't split between us like the enemies hoped but, on the contrary, it united us and made us stronger. The strength of Jews lay just like in the times of Babylon in their spiritual faith; the nation that was formed on an ideological basis and not biological, united by the same altruistic idea, united by the faith in goodness and kindness that can not be taken or broken. We will smile and laugh again, we will dance and sing even louder than ever before and that's how our justice will be done.

May his memory be blessed.

יהי זכרו ברוך

CHAPTER 13

THE LATE "A" AND "H"

"A" and "H" were a young couple that gave birth to the twins ten months ago. When Hamas invaded their kibbutz, they realized that they should hide the kids in the shelter. They took the babies and hid them in the attic determined to protect them with their bodies.

Their mother "H" asked them to keep quiet till she came and they unconsciously realized that they should be silent. The babies survived for 12 long hours without food or water realizing that that's the only way to be saved. The gentle babies proved stronger than the huge monsters, the cowards attacking the weak.

"H" and "A" were barbarically murdered protecting the babies and already had to leave them; they asked permission to give them just one last hug before going into the eternal journey. They were really sad that they would not see them growing, falling in love, or having kids. But they got a promise that they will be able to come for a visit and make sure the kids are taken care of.

They were already far away, in a place full of pure and endless love and hatred that doesn't exist there; the spiritual world, ruled by laws contrary to ours, the world where wild animals live in peace with carnivores and the colorful giant peacocks are listening to the fairies playing on the arches. The pictures of the magic trees and gardens were changing each other, the most spectacular views were opening to their eyes, but all that did not relieve the shooting pain of leaving their kids behind.

NEVER AGAIN

CHAPTER 14

THE LATE AMAZING YOUNG WOMAN

"Do you know that there is an angel floating around you?", he asked her.

"Every person has an angel-a good one and an evil one, depending on what you are choosing at any particular moment of your life", she answered.

"That's simple? Just good and bad, nothing in between?", he asked again.

"That's the whole magic. When you stop justifying evil, you will understand.

There you will find God", said N and closed the door to darkness.

The late "N" was a gorgeous 20-year-old young woman who came to celebrate peace with her friends at the music festival in Reim. When the barbaric terrorists attacked her, she was with her boyfriend but that did not stop them. They raped her one by another just in front of his eyes to make him suffer and humiliate them both. When her legs were finally broken and she could already feel nothing, they hung her on a tree like a trophy.

When her soul left her body, she could barely look at this horrific picture, refusing to believe that she was tormented like that in her own country, in the country they established so that it would never happen again, but "never again" was now. "N" refused to go up, she wanted to return to her parents and her boyfriend who was supposed to become her husband soon, they had already started planning the wedding, and they wanted to have kids.

The angels went down, covering her gently with their mild wings and promising that she would come back again, fulfilling all her dreams next time. But she was still mad that none of her brothers was there, asking to give her at least the last honor and to read the Jewish prayer, Kadish. God himself went down, fulfilling her last wish and returning her soul to the spiritual home of all Jewish souls of the World.

CHAPTER 15

A WHOLE HEART

The late "M" was a Golani fighter, who was one of the first soldiers to fight the terrorists. He saw the terrorists throwing a grenade on the tank with his friends. At this moment, "M", an allegedly gentle young man, didn't think about himself, jumped on the explosive device, and saved his friends. His last words were: "I love you Israel ". He sacrificed himself to save others and by doing so fulfilled the greatest commandment.

The late "T" was in the last stages of pregnancy when Hamas shot her body. The doctors managed to take the baby from her bleeding belly, its tiny body absorbed the bullets, trying to protect her dead mother. The doctors tried to recover her but it was too late, the baby died in their arms, neither seeing the light of the day nor having a name.

"M" saved 13 injured people under the fire. She rescued her life for others by putting their lives first. She was mentally injured and earned the eternal blessing. All those heroes show examples of the only eternal truth, delivered to us by Abraham: "Love your friend as yourself", the truth we inherited genetically from our great grandfather. These people loved their friends more than themselves because they found the divine part in them, it was the creator that they loved so much.

Since this horrible massacre and forever, all the pure souls that were slaughtered barbarically became angels that walk beyond us, inside us. They supervise that we stand together stronger than any fence in the world just as we did during the tragedy in the face of common evil. But this time, they remind us that we should go hand in hand just because we simply can not do otherwise; our brotherhood unites us and thus, brings us closer to the creator, making us similar and equal to the upper force. Those angels make sure we stand like a rock and thus our national resilience, woven of our hearts, becomes our shield and sword that protects us stronger than any other weapon or a wall.

Different countries worldwide that always condemned Israel and appealed its right for existence, sympathized with us. We could see the lights of David on the Eiffel Tower, on the German Parliament of Bundestag, in Western Europe, and more. This light is still very pale and might turn off at any time or, on the contrary, it might shine brightly again with enormous strength.

Jewish destiny is the destiny of the world, we were chosen to fulfill the unique and holy mission-to repair the world, to set an example, and to bring light to the nations worldwide. We were chosen not because of our skin, eyes, or hair color, we were chosen because of the unique faith and spirit that we had on Mount Sinai and that's our eternal mission, whether we want it or not, till we build the spiritual home for all nations in the world, till we become one whole heart again.

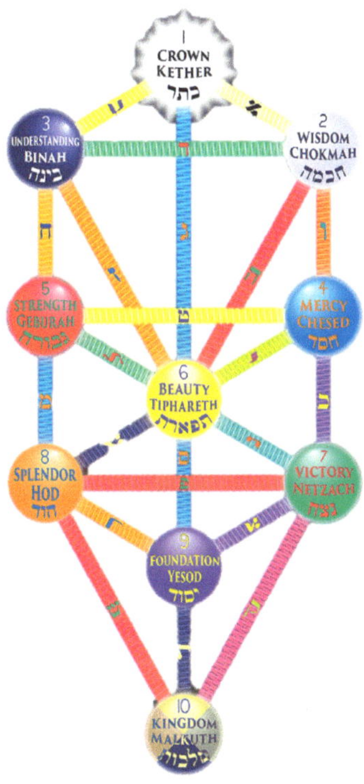

You Got an Invitation to the world of Pure Unconditional love

Acknowledgments

Dedicated to all soldiers of Israel falling heroically or being physically or mentally injured protecting this country.

Thank you, my dear husband, for never stopping to believe in me even in the darkest moments of my life, special thanks to Dr. Oded Ben Haim and Dr. Dan Burla, without you I would never see the world again and would not write this book.

Thank you Rav Michael Laitman, and Lubavitcher Rebbe for enlightening me with Kabbalistic wisdom and Judaism.

Thank you, "Niv Books", for helping me to fulfill my dream and follow my heart. And, of course, all those people who were there for me no matter what. I could constantly feel your support and you became a great source of inspiration in my journey called life.

Despite everything I have been through, I still didn't lose hope in humanity.

I even more strongly believe in miracles and know that there is nothing else but Him.

"Life is not about waiting for the storm to pass, it's about learning how to dance in the rain".

— Vivian Green